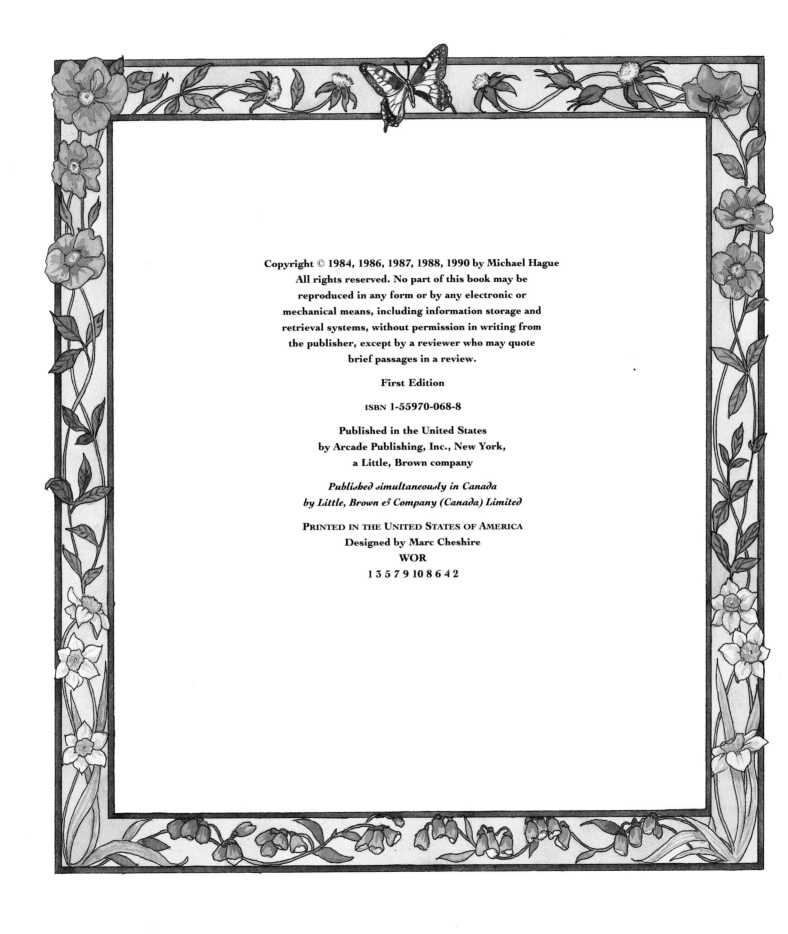

First Edition

ISBN 1-55970-068-8

Published in the United States
by Arcade Publishing, Inc., New York,
a Little, Brown company

Published simultaneously in Canada
by Little, Brown & Company (Canada) Limited

PRINTED IN THE UNITED STATES OF AMERICA
Designed by Marc Cheshire
WOR
1 3 5 7 9 10 8 6 4 2

A UNICORN JOURNAL

Illuminated by

MICHAEL HAGUE

Arcade Publishing — *New York*

Little, Brown and Company